The
WITCH
Who Loved to Make
Children Cry

Denis Bond

Illustrated by
Valeria Petrone

Little
Hippo

Look out for more great titles
by Denis Bond and Valeria Petrone
from Little Hippo!

The Dragon Who Couldn't Help Breathing Fire
The Granny Who Wasn't Like Other Grannies
The Monster Who Couldn't Scare Anyone
The Train Who Was Frightened Of the Dark
The Shark Who Bit Things He Shouldn't

Scholastic Children's Books,
Commonwealth House, 1-19 New Oxford Street,
London WC1A 1NU, UK
a division of Scholastic Ltd

London ~ New York ~ Toronto ~ Sydney ~ Auckland
Mexico City ~ New Delhi ~ Hong Kong

First published in the UK in 1996 by
Scholastic Children's Books
This edition published in 1999 by Little Hippo,
an imprint of Scholastic Ltd

ISBN 0 590 11228 7

Printed in Italy by Amadeus S.p.A. - Rome

In a cottage, deep in a dark forest,
lived a witch.
She was a nasty old witch.
She loved to make children cry.

As the witch flew across the playground on her magic broomstick, she saw children playing.

"I'll go and spoil their fun," cackled the witch. "That'll make them cry." The witch *loved* to make children cry.

The children were laughing excitedly as they went round and round on the huge roundabout. The witch peered through the railings at them and cackled loudly. Then she pointed a long, bony finger at them.

Suddenly, the roundabout began to speed up.
It went *much* faster. *Very* fast. Far *too* fast.
"Help!" cried the terrified children, as they clung on tightly. "We're going to fall off!" Round and round went the roundabout. Round and round and round.

Much, much later, when the
roundabout had finally stopped, the
children staggered off.
They were all feeling very sick.
One small boy was crying.
"Goody, goody, goody," laughed the
witch. "That was great fun!"

The children angrily shook their fists at the witch, who WHOOSHED into the air on her broomstick. "She's always spoiling our fun!" grumbled a little girl.

Later that week, all the children gathered at the top of the hill for the kite competition. And as all the kites floated and danced in the gentle breeze, the little girl laughed excitedly. "Ours is the best kite here," she said.

"It most certainly *is*," agreed the judge as she strolled towards the children, carrying a shiny silver cup in her hand. She wanted to give the cup as a prize to the children who'd made this *beautiful* kite.

"Well done, children!" the judge
shouted. "That must have first prize.
It's the best kite here!"
"It *was* the best kite here," cackled
the witch as she hovered overhead
on her broomstick.
Then she pointed a long, bony finger
into the air.

The gentle breeze suddenly turned into a strong gust of wind, startling everyone. And as all the children were lifted off their feet, they clung desperately to their kite strings. "Oh, no! It's the witch again!" screamed the small boy.

When the wind finally dropped,
everyone stared at their broken kite
strings. There was no sign of any of
the kites. They'd all been blown
away!
The children burst into tears . . .
which pleased the witch
enormously!

"Please go away," pleaded the little girl. "Why are you doing this to us?"

"Aaaaah, have I made you cry?" asked the witch. Then she laughed. "Goody, goody, goody. I *love* to make children cry!"

And she ZOOMED off into the distance.

The next day, the witch perched in a tree in the children's garden. She watched them having a great time in their blow-up paddling pool. "I'll soon spoil their fun," she grinned as she pointed her long, bony finger at the paddling pool.

BANG! Hissssssss! went the paddling pool as it burst and went down. The water and the children tumbled out on to the lawn.

"It's that witch again!" yelled the little girl.

"Why doesn't she leave us alone?" added the small boy.

The witch followed the children everywhere. She followed them to the park and watched them from the bushes as they spread out their picnic. "I hope she doesn't spoil our fun today," said the small boy as he nibbled on a peanut-butter sandwich. The witch pointed her long, bony finger towards the bright blue sky.

Suddenly, a large, black cloud appeared. With a flash of lightning and a crack of thunder, rain fell from the cloud, soaking the children . . . and their crisps . . . and their cakes . . . and their peanut-butter sandwiches.

The children hurried across the park, carrying their picnic things. Everyone, except the little girl, was crying. *She* was very, very angry. "We've got to stop her!" she shouted. The witch watched them. "Aaaaah, they're crying again," she said, softly. Then she laughed. "Goody, goody, goody."

The children sheltered under the old bandstand, waiting for the rain to stop. They saw the witch, leaning over the railings of the duckpond. She was happily feeding the ducks. The witch didn't like children, but she liked ducks.

When the witch turned around, she was horrified to see that her broomstick had gone. She ran along the banks of the duckpond, scaring the ducks and the geese and the swans. "Where is it?" she screeched. "WHERE IS IT?"

The children sat in the bushes,
giggling and watching the witch,
who was frantically searching the
rubbish bins for her lost broomstick.
She looked very upset.
"Serves her right," said the little
girl, who was clutching the magic
broomstick in her hand.

When the witch saw the park-keeper, sweeping the path with his very own broomstick, she rushed at him, angrily.

"You've pinched my broomstick!" she yelled. "Give it back or I'll . . . I'll turn you into a frog!" The terrified park-keeper *immediately* handed it to her. He didn't want to be a frog!

The witch wanted to go home . . .
but the broomstick wouldn't fly.
She tried leaping with it from the
treetops.
But first she landed in the duckpond.

Then she landed in the sandpit.

Finally, she landed in a great pile of
smelly, squelchy manure.

The very sad witch had to travel home on the number nineteen bus. She was very wet. And she was covered in sand and smelly, squelchy manure.

Everyone stared and pointed at the strange, scruffy old woman.

One old man held his nose. "Ugh! What a terrible pong!" he said.

Back in the cottage, in the dark forest, the witch was getting ready for bed.

"My broomstick has lost its magic," she said. "I'll never be able to do *witchy* things again!" And she burst into tears.

Early next morning, the little girl, feeling very ashamed, arrived at the witch's door. Her dad was with her. "I'm sorry," said the little girl. "It's wrong to steal, so I've brought your broomstick back. But you really did upset us."

The witch's face lit up. "Thank you for bringing it back!" she said. "*Thank you.* Goody, goody, goody."

That weekend, the children were riding on the very old merry-go-round horses at the fairground. Suddenly they heard a loud WHOOSH and a high-pitched CACKLE. Then they gasped in horror as they saw the witch ZOOM down from the sky.

"Oh, no," sighed the little girl.
"Here we go again!"
"Please! Please! Please!" cried the
small boy. "Go away. Leave us
alone!"
The witch grinned, cackled again
and pointed her long, bony finger at
the merry-go-round . . .

Suddenly the horses turned into spaceships and flying saucers. They left the merry-go-round and sped upwards, where they WHOOSHED and VROOMED through the sky, miles above the fairground. "WHEEE!" shrieked the children, excitedly. "This is magic!"

And "WHEEE!" went the witch as she joined them, riding on a lightning bolt. "WHEEE! I never knew my magic could be such fun!" The children and the witch had a wonderful time as they ZOOMED and VROOMED across the sky. They laughed and laughed and laughed.

At the end of the day, as they all tucked into enormous, magic-sized ice-creams, the witch said sweetly, "I *love* to make children laugh." And as the delicious ice-cream dribbled down her hairy chin, she sighed, softly, "Mmmm . . . goody, goody, goody."